Zoe's Rescue Zoo

With special thanks to Natalie Doherty

To Mum and Craig, Dad and Jackie x

Text Copyright © 2015 by Hothouse Fiction
Illustrations Copyright © 2015 by Sophy Williams

All rights reserved. Published by Scholastic Inc., 557 Broadway, New York, NY 10012, *Publishers since 1920.* SCHOLASTIC and associated logos are trademarks and/or registered trademarks of Scholastic Inc. Published by arrangement with Nosy Crow Ltd. Series created by Hothouse Fiction.

First published in the United Kingdom in 2013 by Nosy Crow Ltd., The Crow's Nest, 10a Lant St., London, SE1 1QR.

The publisher does not have any control over and does not assume any responsibility for author or third-party websites or their content.

ISBN 978-0-545-84222-8

10 9   17 18 19/0

Printed in the U.S.A.   40
First edition, September 2015

Book design by Mary Claire Cruz

Zoe's Rescue Zoo

The Puzzled Penguin

Amelia Cobb

Illustrated by Sophy Williams

Scholastic Inc.

Chapter One
Summer at the Rescue Zoo!

Zoe Parker grinned as she ran out of the school gates, swinging her bag beside her. Her mom was waiting for her. "It's summer vacation!" Zoe yelled, giving her mom a big hug.

Her mom smiled and ruffled her daughter's wavy brown hair. "How was the last day of school?" she asked.

Zoe began to skip excitedly along the sidewalk. "It was fun, but I just couldn't wait for vacation to start." She smiled at her mom. "And I get to spend every single day at my favorite place."

As they got closer to home Zoe heard noises ahead: roars, bellows, screeches, and squeaks. Animal noises!

Finally they turned a corner, and there in front of them stood a pair of tall, beautiful gates with a line of lush oak trees on either side. The gates were made of golden wood and covered with delicate carvings of every sort of animal you could think of. There were majestic tigers, soaring eagles, snapping crocodiles, and elegant gazelles. About halfway up, two words were carved across the gates in swirling letters: RESCUE ZOO. Right at the

top, a golden hot-air balloon twinkled in
the sunlight.

A line of excited visitors was streaming
through the gates, but Zoe and her
mom walked right past them. As she
stepped inside the zoo, a familiar warm,
happy feeling spread through Zoe's
stomach. "Home sweet home," she
whispered.

Zoe and her mom weren't visiting
the zoo — they *lived* there! Zoe's Great-
Uncle Horace was a famous explorer and
animal expert, and on his travels around
the world he had met lots of animals in
need of help. That was why he'd decided
to build the zoo, so it could be a safe
place for any creature who was lost,
injured, or in trouble. Now it was home
to hundreds of amazing animals!

Zoe's mom was Horace's niece and the zoo vet. She and Zoe lived in a little cottage on the edge of the zoo, so Zoe's mom could be there whenever the animals needed her. Zoe couldn't imagine a better place to live!

Beyond the gates, a redbrick path wound its way through the zoo. On a warm summer's day like this, there were hundreds of visitors, chattering as they

wandered past each enclosure. Now that school had finished, lots of families were starting to arrive. Zoe spotted Jack and Nicola from her class, still in their green-and-white school uniforms. She smiled and waved at them, and they waved back.

"That's Zoe, the girl I told you about," she heard Jack telling his dad. "She lives here. It's so cool!"

As Zoe and her mom made their way through the crowds to their cottage, Zoe heard an excited chattering noise above her. She looked up, shading her eyes from the bright sunlight. From the top of a sycamore tree, a furry face peeked down at her.

"Meep!" called Zoe, smiling. "Come down from there, you silly thing!"

With a swift leap, the little creature bounded down and landed nimbly on Zoe's shoulder. Zoe gathered the soft, warm bundle into her arms for a hug. Meep was a tiny gray mouse lemur with enormous golden eyes and a long, velvety tail. Great-Uncle Horace had rescued him when he was just a baby and had brought him to the Rescue Zoo. Now Meep lived in the cottage with Zoe and was her very best friend.

"Meep has been especially mischievous today," Zoe's mom told her as they continued along the path. "Mr. Pinch brought in a very tasty-looking blueberry muffin this morning for his breakfast. Then this week's fruit delivery arrived, and he went to supervise it. When he came back, his muffin was gone. Mr. Pinch was *very* upset." Zoe's mom shook her head at the little lemur. "He didn't know what had happened to it, but *I* noticed that Meep's paws were covered in crumbs!"

Zoe couldn't help laughing and hugged Meep closer. Mr. Pinch was the zoo

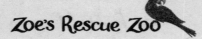

manager, and was *always* grumpy. Meep loved teasing him!

As they arrived at the cottage, Zoe's mom handed Zoe her school bag. "I have to go and check on a leopard now, so I'll leave you two to have fun. Be home in time for dinner." She planted a quick kiss on Zoe's head and tickled Meep's soft little belly.

"OK, Mom!" Zoe smiled as she watched her dash away toward the zoo hospital.

Once Zoe's mom was out of sight, Zoe stepped inside the cottage and grinned at Meep. The mischievous little lemur leaped from her shoulder and scampered over to the bowl of fruit on the kitchen table.

"Yummy!" he chirped, peeling a banana with his nimble fingers. "Blueberry muffins are nice, but I like bananas best."

Zoe giggled. It
was always fun to
be alone with
Meep or any of
the animals at
the Rescue
Zoo. When
other people
weren't around,
she didn't have to
hide their amazing secret.

Zoe knew that animals could talk to
people, and that just a few special people
could talk back to them. And she was one
of them!

Chapter Two
Mr. Pinch's Plan

Zoe dashed upstairs to get changed. She picked out a bright-yellow sundress and her favorite blue flip-flops and quickly rubbed some sunscreen into her cheeks. Then she fastened a pretty silver necklace around her neck. This was a very special necklace. It had a charm shaped like a paw print, and it had been a present

from Great-Uncle Horace. The
paw-print charm opened every single
gate in the Rescue Zoo, so Zoe could see
any of the animals whenever she wanted!

Meep perched on her bed. "Zoe, do
you really not have to go to school
tomorrow?" the little lemur asked
hopefully.

Zoe smiled at Meep in her bedroom
mirror. "No, Meep. No school for *two
whole months,* so I can spend lots of time
with you!"

Meep squeaked happily, bouncing up
and down on the bed.

Zoe slid a yellow butterfly clip into
her hair and turned to face her friend.
"It's good I'm here to stop you from doing
troublesome things, like eating Mr. Pinch's
breakfast! You shouldn't take things that

don't belong to you,
Meep. You're lucky
he didn't spot you."

Meep leaped
into her arms
for a hug.
"But it was
funny, Zoe.
And delicious!"

Zoe
couldn't help
smiling. Meep was so adorable that she
found everything he did cute — even
when he was getting in trouble. She
stroked his soft ears gently and lifted him
up to her shoulder.

"Come on, Meep. Let's go and see
what's going on in the zoo!"

Zoe and Meep raced outside and

12

weaved through the bustle of visitors
until they reached a little path between
the llamas and the porcupines. Tall beech
trees stretched overhead, shading the path
from the warm sun. Zoe knew all the
shortcuts around the Rescue Zoo, and this
pretty path was always one of the quietest
places. With fewer visitors around, she
and Meep could chat as much as they
wanted!

"Let's go and see the hippos first," Zoe
suggested. "Little Hetty's learning to swim
at the moment. If we're lucky, we might
catch her while she's splashing around!"

Like all the enclosures at the Rescue
Zoo, the muddy lagoon that Hetty shared
with her mom and sisters was specially
built for them and looked just like a
hippo's home in the wild. Zoe and Meep

loved watching them wallow around, blowing bubbles in the gloopy mud.

As they walked along, Zoe twirled on the path happily. "We can do so many fun things over the summer, Meep," she said. "Every morning we can help give Rory and Leonard their breakfast. And Luna is going to have her pups any day now, so we can help look after them. I've never seen arctic wolf cubs before."

Meep wriggled excitedly. "I hope Goo comes home too, Zoe," he chattered. "I miss him."

Zoe grinned at Meep's nickname for her Great-Uncle Horace. "So do I, Meep. And I hope he brings a new animal for the Rescue Zoo with him! That would make this summer perfect."

As they walked toward Hetty's

14

enclosure, they heard an angry voice grumbling further along the path. "Oh no. Paint on my clean hat!"

"Quick, Meep!" whispered Zoe. "Hide!"

They both darted behind a large cherry tree and peered around it. Just in front of the penguin enclosure was Mr. Pinch, clutching a paintbrush and a can of blue paint. He was painting a sign on a little wooden hut with a pointed roof. There was a drop of blue paint on his hat and he looked very upset. Meep giggled.

A little further down the path,

Zoe's mom came out of the rhinoceros enclosure, her vet's bag slung across her shoulders. She smiled at Mr. Pinch and nodded at the hut. "Hello! You look busy!"

"Hello," Mr. Pinch muttered. "Yes. I seem to be the only one who does anything around here." On Zoe's shoulder, Meep blew a raspberry. "Actually, I'm glad you came this way," Mr. Pinch continued. "I've been meaning to speak to you today. I have a project for your daughter."

Zoe and Meep looked at each other and frowned. What was Mr. Pinch up to? They both stayed very still, trying to hear what he said. Meep's ears quivered curiously.

Zoe's mom glanced at

the wooden hut. "A project? That sounds like fun! Zoe's been so looking forward to spending more time at the zoo now that school's done for the year."

"Hmm. It will definitely keep Zoe and her little . . . er, *friend*, entertained," Mr. Pinch agreed with a smirk. "I thought she could start tomorrow."

Zoe's heart sank. Whatever Mr. Pinch was planning, she knew it wasn't going to be fun! He didn't like Zoe and Meep being allowed to wander around the zoo like all the grown-up staff did, and he'd do anything to ruin her vacation! *Say no, Mom*, she pleaded silently.

Zoe's mom hesitated. "Well . . . I'm sure Zoe will want to help out in any way she can —"

"Excellent!" Mr. Pinch interrupted. "Tell her to be here at nine o'clock sharp. Now, if you'll excuse me, Mrs. Parker, I must keep painting. Lots to do."

He smiled and waved as Zoe's mom walked off down the path, then turned back to the sign he was painting, muttering to himself. "Ha! Fun! This job will keep that pesky girl and her fluffball out

18

of mischief all summer long. Now, that *is* fun!"

Mr. Pinch whistled cheerfully to himself, as Zoe and Meep looked at each other in dismay.

Chapter Three
The Tricky Tickets

The next morning as the zoo gates were opening, Zoe and Meep made their way back to the little wooden hut. When Zoe's mom had told her that Mr. Pinch wanted them to help with a special summer project, Zoe had just nodded sadly.

As they walked along the redbrick path through the zoo, a pair of colorful plum-headed parakeets flew in circles above their heads. Zoe could tell it was going to be a beautiful hot day. From the enclosures around her, different animals squawked, roared, and squeaked in greeting, happy to see her and Meep. Zoe desperately wanted to stop and talk to them all, but she knew she couldn't be late for Mr. Pinch.

It was even harder to keep going when Oscar, the African elephant, saw her and trumpeted in excitement.

"I'm sorry, Oscar," Zoe said miserably, reaching through the fence to stroke his long, wrinkled trunk. "I can't give you your breakfast today. I promise I'll try to visit later on."

Oscar blinked his dark eyes sadly, and then nodded his enormous head to show Zoe he understood.

As they arrived at the hut, Mr. Pinch was already waiting for them. He was holding a small cardboard box under one arm.

"Hello, Mr. Pinch," Zoe said in the most polite voice she could muster. "What would you like us to do?"

Mr. Pinch pointed to the hut. Pictures of penguins had been carefully pasted on the sides, and Mr. Pinch's sign had been finished.

Zoe read it out loud. "PENGUIN FEEDING SHOW. EVERY DAY AT THREE O'CLOCK."

Mr. Pinch nodded importantly. "This summer there will be a new attraction at the Rescue Zoo: a daily penguin feeding show." He made a face. "If you ask *me*, it will be a horrible messy business, but it was Will, the penguin-keeper's, idea. Anyway, it occurred to me that you two would be the perfect pair to sell the tickets." He smiled smugly at them. "After all, I am far too busy to do it myself. I have the entire zoo to run."

Mr. Pinch handed Zoe the cardboard box he was carrying. Zoe lifted the lid warily. The box was packed full of small yellow tickets. Stamped neatly on each one were the words PENGUIN FEEDING SHOW. ADMISSION: ONE.

"Do we have to sell all of these?" Zoe asked. "There are hundreds!"

"A hundred and fifty for each show, to be precise." Mr. Pinch smirked. "There's a chair in the hut so you can sit down, and there's a box to collect the money every time you sell a ticket. You'll be far too

busy to go around the zoo, poking your
nose into things that don't concern you."

Whistling happily, Mr. Pinch strolled off
down the path. Meep
leaped onto the
roof of the little
wooden hut
and blew a
very rude
raspberry at
the grumpy
zookeeper. "Horrible
Mr. Pinch!" he chirped.

Zoe pushed open the door of the hut
and went inside, with Meep scampering
after her. As she sat down behind the
little hatch with the box of tickets on her
lap, she had a sudden, horrible thought.
"Meep, Mr. Pinch said the show was

daily, all through the summer, didn't he?
I think he's going to make us sell tickets
every single day until I go back to
school!"

The lemur squeaked in alarm, his big
eyes wide. Zoe took a deep, shaky breath.
She felt so disappointed. It was as though
Mr. Pinch had just snatched all her plans
and ideas for the summer vacation out
of her hands, and there was nothing she
could do about it.

Just then, a couple walked down the
path with a little girl. Zoe sat up straight
and smiled bravely. "Come on, Meep," she
whispered. "The sooner we sell the tickets,
the sooner we can be back out in the
sunshine having fun!"

The little girl spotted the hut first and
read the sign out loud carefully. "Ooh,

penguins!" she said, tugging at the man's hand. "Daddy, look! Can we go?"

"That sounds like fun," her dad agreed, smiling at Zoe. They started to walk over to the hut, and Zoe practiced what she was going to say in her head. *Three tickets? That's six dollars, please! I hope you enjoy the show.* Maybe this wasn't going to be so hard after all! But before she could say a word, there was a long hooting call from further down the path. It was so loud that the couple gasped and the little girl's eyes went wide. "What was *that*?" she whispered, glancing at Zoe.

"That sounds like Sydney, our siamang gibbon," Zoe explained. "Siamangs are the loudest of all the apes. Sydney's just a baby, but she's very noisy — especially in the morning before breakfast!"

The little girl's face lit up. "Mommy, let's go and see her!"

The family all rushed down the path toward Star's lush forest enclosure.

"Wait!" Zoe called after them as Meep chattered loudly. "Wouldn't you like to buy your tickets first?"

But they were already too far away to hear her. Zoe sighed. "Never mind, Meep," she told her little friend. "We'll sell tickets to the next visitors who come along, you'll see!"

Zoe and Meep tried their best to sell as many tickets as they could — but it was hard work. By 12:30 the stack of yellow tickets didn't seem any smaller than when they'd started. "We've only sold . . . eleven," Zoe said, glancing worriedly at the pile of bills in the money box.

28

"That's not very many," grumbled Meep.

Zoe gathered her little friend into her arms for a cuddle. "I think the problem is that there are too many amazing animals to see at the Rescue Zoo. Hardly any visitors have stopped at our hut because they're all rushing to see Star or the orangutans or the lions or the dolphins. They're just having too much fun to buy our tickets!"

Chapter Four
Making a Splash!

"Cheer up, you two!" a friendly voice called.

Zoe's mom was walking down the path toward them, a large brown paper bag under her arm. "Come out and get some sunshine. I've brought you a picnic lunch."

"Yum! My stomach's rumbling. I knew

30

it must be lunchtime!" chirped Meep as he scampered through the hatch.

Zoe's mom handed the paper bag to Zoe, gave her a hug, and continued on to see her next patient. Zoe and Meep dashed through the zoo to their favorite picnic spot: a sunny stretch of grass overlooking a wide, glittering lake where the dolphins swam.

The little lemur was so excited about the picnic, he started leaping around in circles on the grass, spilling his lunch.

"You're dropping seeds everywhere, Meep!" Zoe laughed, shaking her head at her funny friend. She sighed as she finished her sandwich. "I wish we could stay out here all day, Meep," she said wistfully. "Now that we're in the sunshine, it's going to be even harder to go back inside the hut."

As Zoe began to gather up the leftovers
from their picnic, she felt a sudden ripple
of excitement run through the zoo. On
the path behind her, there was a new
burst of chatter among the visitors. Across
the sparkling lake, the springboks had all
stopped grazing and were standing alert,
their slender ears pricked up. The dolphins
swam up to the surface and lifted their
gray heads into the air, clicking happily.
Zoe could hear Star calling
loudly, and in the

aviary nearby, hundreds of birds had started to squawk and hoot. Even Meep was gazing up into the sky, his soft ears quivering gently. "Listen!" he chirped.

Over the sudden noise of the animals, Zoe could hear a low, distant buzzing sound. It gradually grew louder and louder. Suddenly she recognized the sound, and a huge grin spread across her face.

Meep leaped onto her shoulder. "Zoe! Zoe!" the little lemur squeaked, bouncing up and down. "He's back! Goo's back!"

Zoe hugged Meep as a small red
seaplane appeared on the horizon, flying
low over the zoo. As the plane soared
over each different enclosure, Zoe could
hear the animals stamping their hooves,
fluttering their wings, and swishing their
tails. Every creature was welcoming home
the Rescue Zoo's owner!

As the plane reached the lake and began to drop down onto the water, Zoe jumped to her feet, waving wildly. With a big splash, the plane glided onto the surface and skimmed through the water toward the shore.

A growing crowd of visitors and zookeepers gathered around, including Zoe's mom. "I ran all the way from the zoo hospital when I saw the plane!" she told Zoe, panting. The plane's door was flung open, and Zoe grinned as she saw Great-Uncle Horace's familiar face, beaming at her from the cockpit. His bushy white hair was covered up by a large, fleecy hat, and a spotted scarf was wrapped around his neck.

Perched on his shoulder was a big, beautiful bird, with glossy feathers of a

35

rich, deep blue. Kiki was a
hyacinth macaw. Great-
Uncle Horace had
rescued her years ago,
when she was just
a tiny ball of fluffy
feathers, and they
were as close as Zoe
and Meep were.

Kiki squawked a
greeting at Zoe and fluffed
up her feathers haughtily when she saw
Meep. The little lemur was often rude
to the proud old macaw, and they weren't
the best of friends!

Great-Uncle Horace climbed out of the
plane, and Zoe, her mom, and Meep
rushed to meet him.

Zoe's mom laughed as she hugged her

uncle. "We've missed you!" she told him. "It's great to have you back."

Great-Uncle Horace winked at Zoe. "It's very nice to be here in the sunshine! Kiki and I have just come from somewhere very cold and snowy indeed — the Antarctic! That's where the South Pole is, you know. Goodness, Zoe, what a fascinating place it is. Did you know that there is no land whatsoever at the South Pole — just ice? And no animals live there, because it's just too chilly for them." He beamed at Zoe. "But there are many, many different creatures living in the cold blue water. Kiki and I met a school of humpback whales and a very friendly pod of seals. We even saw a blue whale!"

"Did you bring an animal home, Great-Uncle Horace?" Zoe asked eagerly.

She tried standing on her tiptoes to see inside the plane.

Great-Uncle Horace laughed softly. "As a matter of fact, I did."

He reached carefully inside the plane and picked up a small wooden crate from the backseat. There was a tiny peeping sound coming from inside it. Great-Uncle Horace placed it gently on the ground and lifted the lid. Then he reached inside and gathered a fluffy bundle into his arms.

Zoe gasped, and there was a murmur from the crowd behind her. She took a tentative step forward. "He's so small," she whispered. "Mom, Meep, look!"

Huddled in a warm blanket, and blinking curiously at the crowd, was a beautiful baby penguin!

Chapter Five
The New Arrival

The penguin chick was tiny with a
velvety black head. His fluffy little body
was pale gray and looked as soft as a
stuffed animal.

He stared right at Zoe, and Zoe stared
back. There was a penguin colony at
the Rescue Zoo, so Zoe had met lots
of penguins before — but all the zoo

penguins were grown up, and none were as adorable as this one!

Great–Uncle Horace smiled at her. "He's only three weeks old," he explained. "I've named him Pip. He's an emperor penguin."

Zoe's mom examined Pip carefully. "He's beautiful, Uncle Horace," she said. "But what happened to him? Where is his family?"

Great–Uncle Horace nodded. "It's a long story, my dear. I promise to tell you all about it later."

"Can I pet him?" Zoe asked hopefully. She knew it wasn't always a good idea to touch a wild animal, especially one that had only just arrived at the zoo, but Pip looked so friendly.

Great–Uncle Horace smiled. "Of

course, Zoe," he told her. "Just be very
gentle."

Zoe reached out tentatively and
touched Pip's fluffy little belly. She didn't
think she'd ever felt anything so soft. As
she stroked him, the little chick opened his
beak and made a happy peeping sound.

"Aha!" said Great-Uncle Horace. "You've
discovered he likes to be tickled! Now, let's
see if the little fellow wants to explore."

He placed Pip carefully on the ground
in front of him. The little
chick gazed around for a
moment, then waddled
right over to Great-
Uncle Horace's side
and rubbed his head
happily against his leg.

"He's certainly very

attached to you!" Zoe's mom told her
uncle, smiling down at Pip. "I think it
might be best if he stays with you for now.
He might be frightened if we take him
away too quickly. We can introduce
him to the other penguins and his new
home tomorrow."

Great-Uncle Horace nodded wisely.
"Very sensible, my dear, as always. I'll
keep the little guy with me tonight.
I'll be leaving again tomorrow afternoon,
so we should make sure he's settled
before I go."

Zoe felt a rush of disappointment.
*Tomorrow? But Great-Uncle Horace had been
away for* weeks. *Did he really have to leave
again so soon?* She glanced sadly at Meep,
who leaped from her shoulder into her
arms for a cuddle. Zoe knew the little

lemur had missed
Great-Uncle Horace
almost as much as
she had, and
they'd both
hoped he'd
be staying
at the zoo
longer.

Great-Uncle Horace smiled at her
kindly. "I'm sorry, Zoe. But I've already
gotten a message about another animal
who needs my help — a dolphin at the
Great Barrier Reef who's hurt his flipper
on a piece of coral."

Zoe's mom put her arm around Zoe
and gave her a reassuring hug. "In that
case, you and Kiki have to come to the
cottage for dinner this evening," she told

Great-Uncle Horace. "Pip too, of course. I want to hear all about how you rescued him, and I'm sure Zoe does too!"

"I'd be delighted, my dear," replied Great-Uncle Horace. "What a treat! And I'm looking forward to hearing all *your* news too. Now, it's time for me to pay a visit to the other animals. I know they'll be expecting me."

Great-Uncle Horace trotted away down the path with Pip in his arms and Kiki soaring above them. The crowds began to scatter in different directions, talking excitedly.

Zoe's mom gave Zoe a kiss before heading back to the zoo hospital. "Good luck with the tickets this afternoon," she said, smiling. "See you at dinnertime. Be good, Meep!"

Zoe skipped back along the path to the hut, her mind buzzing with all the news she wanted to tell Great-Uncle Horace that evening and the questions she would ask about Pip. Meep scampered along beside her, squeaking excitedly.

"Did you see how teeny he was, Zoe?" the little lemur chattered, his big eyes wide. "Almost as small as me!"

As they pushed open the door of the hut and went back inside, Zoe realized she didn't even mind. Today was turning out much better than she had imagined. Great-Uncle Horace was back, and the Rescue Zoo had a wonderful new animal. Not even Mr. Pinch could ruin that!

Chapter Six
Penguin Rescue

When Zoe opened the cottage door that evening, she grinned as she breathed in delicious cooking smells. Her mom was lifting a big, bubbling lasagna out of the oven.

Great-Uncle Horace was already sitting at the table, nibbling a piece of garlic bread and feeding crumbs to Kiki, who was perched on his shoulder.

As Zoe kicked off her flip-flops and stepped into the kitchen, she heard a tiny scrambling sound and looked down. Pip came waddling across the kitchen tiles and stood right in front of her, staring up very seriously.

"It looks like you've made a friend," Great-Uncle Horace commented as the little penguin rubbed his tiny head against Zoe's leg — just as he had done to Great-Uncle Horace earlier.

"Come and sit down, Zoe," her mom said. "It's lasagna and salad for us, and nuts and berries for Kiki and Meep."

"What about Pip?" Zoe asked, sitting down and grabbing a piece of garlic bread.

"Well, in the wild, baby penguins are

too small to find food for themselves,"
Great-Uncle Horace explained. "When
they are first born, they usually eat fish
that their mom or dad has chewed up
into a soft mush for them. When I first
found little Pip, I mushed up fish for him
with a fork. Now he's big enough for fish
and krill, like the Rescue Zoo penguins."
He held up a little blue box. "Will was
kind enough to give me a few krill from
the penguin colony's food supply."

Zoe made a face and Meep wrinkled
his nose, as Horace showed them the tiny,
silvery prawns inside the box.

"I'm glad I'm having nuts!" Meep said
to Zoe as he nibbled a peanut.

Great-Uncle Horace placed the box on
the table and sat the little chick on his lap.
Then he chose a tiny krill and held it in

front of Pip. The little penguin gobbled it
up, peeping happily.

Zoe giggled. "Can I try?" she asked.
Great-Uncle Horace nodded kindly.
"We'll take turns."

"Now, Uncle Horace," Zoe's mom said,
"you have to tell us about how you found
the chick."

Great-Uncle Horace smiled fondly at Pip. "The little guy was very lucky," he explained. "You see, I had traveled to the South Pole to investigate a squid with tangled tentacles. Thankfully, I was able to untie the poor fellow right away, and Kiki and I were just about to fly off. As I started the engine, smart Kiki started squawking as noisily as she could!" He beamed at the beautiful macaw, who fluffed up her feathers proudly.

"I always say Kiki is my lucky charm," Great-Uncle Horace continued, "and she proved me right. She had spotted something on the ice, so we went to have a closer look."

"And it was a baby penguin!" said Zoe.

"You're almost right!" Great-Uncle Horace chuckled. "It was a single egg,

alone on the ice. And just a few moments
later, our little friend hatched! I wrapped
him in a cozy blanket and tucked him
safely in the plane. Adult penguins love
the cold, of course, because they're covered
in warm feathers that keep them nice and
dry. But penguin chicks only have a light,
fluffy layer of down, so they need to be
kept warm until their feathers grow."

"But where was his family?" Zoe
asked. "I thought baby penguins huddle
up underneath their parents so they don't
get cold."

Great-Uncle Horace suddenly looked
very sad. "I don't know, my dear. But
in the Antarctic, there are much bigger
creatures than penguins. I'm afraid they
were gone for good." He sighed. "That's
why I decided Pip had to come back

to the Rescue Zoo. Left there alone, he would never have survived."

Zoe gazed at the little chick. *He lost his family before he was even born*, she thought sadly. *But at least he's safe now.*

Great-Uncle Horace yawned loudly. "Goodness, I do apologize!" he said. "I think it must be bedtime for me. It has been a very long day. I need to get some rest."

Great-Uncle Horace helped Zoe carry the empty dishes to the kitchen sink and then gathered the little penguin gently into his arms. "Come along, young fellow. It's time for you to get some sleep too!" he told the chick.

They all went to the door to say good-bye. Outside, the sky had turned a beautiful dusky purple with a scattering of stars. In the distance, a manor house stood high on a hill, overlooking the zoo. A cluster of windows were lit up, making the house look warm and inviting. This was Higgins Hall, Great-Uncle Horace's house.

Great-Uncle Horace kissed Zoe and her mom good-night and stroked

Meep's head, which made
Kiki squawk angrily.
"Sleep well!" Zoe
said, smiling.
"I'm sure we
will, my dear. Did
you know that
emperor penguins
sleep standing up
with their beaks
tucked underneath
a flipper?" Great-
Uncle Horace smiled
down at the sleepy penguin. He
winked at Zoe and lowered his voice
to a whisper. "Kiki does tend to snore
quite loudly. Let's hope the little guy
doesn't mind!"

Zoe smiled as Great-Uncle Horace

picked up the little penguin. Zoe bent
down and stroked his soft, fluffy little
head. He blinked curiously up at her. *I
wish I could speak to you now*, she thought.
But I have to wait until we're on our own!

Chapter Seven
The Puzzled Penguin

"What are your plans for this fine day, my dear?" Great-Uncle Horace asked Zoe the next morning. Zoe and Meep had rushed over to Higgins Hall to see him and Pip as soon as they woke up.

Zoe quickly explained about selling tickets for the penguin-feeding show.

Great-Uncle Horace patted Zoe's hand

reassuringly. "Oh, dear. Percy Pinch can be a little bossy, I'm afraid. Anyway, that gives me an excellent idea!" he went on. "As the hut is next to the penguin enclosure, maybe you could take Pip with you and introduce him to Will and the rest of the colony. Would you do that for me?" He smiled down at the chick. "The little fellow has become rather attached to me, and it's going to be hard to say good-bye. I'd feel so much happier knowing *you* were taking care of him, my dear."

"Of course!" said Zoe. This would give her the chance to be alone with Pip, so she could talk to him. And she couldn't wait to see the chick's reaction when he saw the amazing penguin enclosure!

Great-Uncle Horace bent down to give Pip a good-bye tickle. "Enjoy your new home, little one. I know Zoe here will look after you very well."

Zoe and Meep set off down the path with her mom and Great-Uncle Horace waving from the doorway. The little penguin looked back at Great-Uncle Horace, but he soon waddled after Zoe. Zoe made sure she walked very slowly, so Pip could keep up. He looked so funny, flapping his tiny gray wings as he followed her.

As soon as the house was out of sight, Zoe grinned and knelt down on the path. At last she could talk to the chick! Whenever she spoke to a new animal for the first time, she always made sure she used her quietest, gentlest voice in case they were surprised or frightened. Animals talked to people all the time, of course, but most of them had never heard a person talk back before!

"I'm Zoe," she told him. "This is my best friend, Meep. We're so happy you came to the Rescue Zoo!"

The little penguin gazed at her, his shiny black eyes wide. He fluttered his wings and made a happy cheeping sound.

Zoe smiled. "I've been able to speak to animals since I was little," she explained. "I'm very lucky! You're going to love it here. Just wait until we get to your new home! It's so beautiful. There's a huge iceberg and a lagoon where you can splash around and swim. But best of all, there are lots and lots of other penguins for you to play with!"

The little chick looked puzzled. He waddled closer to Zoe and cheeped curiously. Zoe gasped and Meep chirped in surprise. "I can't believe it," breathed Zoe. "Pip doesn't know what a penguin is!"

Suddenly she realized why the chick might be confused.

"Meep, I think I understand," she said. "Pip's never even *seen* another penguin. When he hatched, his family was already gone. The only creatures he's met are Great-Uncle Horace and Kiki."

Meep wrinkled his nose. "What are we going to do, Zoe?"

Zoe glanced at the little chick. Pip was waddling playfully around in circles, peeping happily. "I think we should continue on to the penguin enclosure,

Meep. Maybe if Pip sees the colony, he'll realize he's one of them."

They arrived at the penguin enclosure five minutes later. Beyond the glass wall there was a deep, open-air lagoon with a glittering iceberg rising out of the cold blue water like an enormous diamond. Most of the penguins were splashing around in the shallow end of the lagoon, staying nice and cool on such a warm summer's day. Pip watched them curiously.

Zoe reached for her necklace and touched the paw-print charm to a small metal panel on the gate. With a click, the gate opened and they all stepped inside.

Zoe spotted Will and waved. The penguin-keeper came rushing over to them, carrying a bucket. "You brought the new arrival!" Will said, grinning. "I've been looking forward to meeting him. Isn't he tiny!"

"His name's Pip," Zoe told him.

"Well, I hope Pip's hungry." Will waved the bucket. "It's breakfast time!"

He walked over to the edge of the lagoon and began throwing handfuls of silvery krill into the water. With a chorus of excited squawks, the penguins swooped gracefully after the fish. Some of them shot through the lagoon so quickly it looked like they were flying underwater.

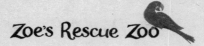

Zoe glanced at Pip. He was watching the other penguins but he hadn't moved from her side.

Will looked at the little chick thoughtfully. "Maybe he's not hungry. Or he might think the other penguins are too fast for him." He held out a krill to the little chick. "Here you go, buddy. This one's just for you!" Pip gobbled it up, flapping his wings happily.

Will laughed. "So he *was* hungry! I've been a penguin-keeper for a long time, and I've never met a penguin who didn't want to get into the water before!"

Zoe nodded. "Would it be OK if I stayed with him for a little while?" she asked.

"Of course, Zoe. No problem. I've got a few jobs to do on the other side of the lagoon, so come and find me if you need anything." Will picked up the empty bucket and strolled off.

Zoe found a seat a little bit further away from the water on a warm, dry piece of rock. Meep scampered onto her shoulder, and Pip waddled after her, staying close. Zoe couldn't help smiling as the chick cuddled up next to her.

"These are all penguins, Pip, like you," she whispered. "See, birds have feathers and wings and beaks, like you." Zoe pointed to Pip's fluffy stomach and little beak. "Humans like me have arms and

legs, and we don't have feathers. Penguins
are birds. Come and meet the others,
then you'll see they're just like you!" Zoe
suggested.

She glanced across
to the other side
of the lagoon,
making sure
Will was too
far away to
hear her, and
then called out
softly to them.
"Pearl! Poppy!
Come over here — there's
someone I'd like you to meet!"

The penguins were gliding quickly
under the surface of the lagoon. Their
flippers were tucked in neatly and

their sleek, shiny bodies wriggled as they
swam faster and faster. With a sudden
splash, they launched themselves out of
the water and into the air. They landed

on their white bellies on the smooth rocks
and slid playfully along. Pearl and Poppy
shook the water from their bodies and
waddled over followed by the rest of the
colony.

"This is Pip, everyone," Zoe explained.
"Great-Uncle Horace brought him back
to the Rescue Zoo yesterday from the

South Pole. He was all by himself, so we need to take extra special care of him."

Pip gazed solemnly up at the older birds who flapped their wings and made excited squawking sounds, welcoming the little chick.

"You looked as if you were having lots of fun in the water this morning," Zoe said to the penguins. "Why don't you take Pip for a swim?"

Poppy fluttered her tail feathers eagerly and leaped right back into the lagoon to show Pip how easy it was. Zoe giggled.

But the little chick wouldn't leave Zoe's side. When Pearl and Poppy tried to encourage him to follow them into the lagoon, Pip covered his eyes with a flipper and shook his head.

Zoe bent down to listen to what he was

saying. "You know you're not a penguin because you can't swim? But, Pip, I'm sure you can, you just have to practice!"

But Pip shook his head again. Eventually the penguins gave up and jumped back into the water. Zoe was very disappointed — she'd been so sure that Pip would love his new home, but he just didn't want to join in.

"What do we do now, Zoe?" Meep said anxiously.

Zoe sighed. "I wish we could stay with Pip, but we have to go and sell tickets."

She knelt down in front of the little penguin. "Meep and I have to go now," she explained sadly. "But we'll come back tomorrow, I promise."

She walked toward the gate, but Pip waddled after her. Zoe smiled. "No, this is your home now. You have to stay here."

Pip cheeped and hopped up and down.

Zoe shook her head. "You won't be lonely. You've got all the other penguins to play with. See you soon!" She jumped outside and shut the enclosure door firmly.

Zoe and Meep looked at each other sadly as they heard Pip peeping for them from inside the enclosure. Zoe's heart melted. She flung open the enclosure door and the tiny penguin rushed out so fast he bumped into her legs.

"Yay!" Meep chattered. "Can he live with us?"

Zoe looked determined as Pip hopped up and down happily. "No," she told them. "Pip belongs here with the penguins — and we're going to prove it to him!"

Chapter Eight
Pip the Flamingo!

Zoe set back off into the zoo with Meep
scampering ahead and Pip waddling
behind her.

"What are we going to do, Zoe?"
chattered Meep.

"We're going to take Pip around
the zoo and introduce him to some of the
other animals," Zoe explained. "Maybe

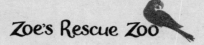
then he'll see that he belongs with the penguins."

The zoo gates had just opened, and the first visitors of the day were streaming inside. Everyone gasped to see the tiny penguin walking along the path, and lots of people pulled out their cameras and started snapping photos.

"Pip, watch out for all these feet. I don't want you to get squashed!" Zoe whispered. "Let's turn on to the next path, it's quieter there."

They passed the rhinos, the peacocks, and the giant tortoise, Charles, who was the Rescue Zoo's oldest animal.

"Which enclosure should we visit first, Zoe?" chirped Meep.

Before Zoe could reply, Pip peeped excitedly and flapped his little wings. He began waddling away very quickly. Zoe frowned and followed him. What had he spotted?

Meep realized which enclosure the chick was heading toward. "He's going to the flamingos!" he said.

The little chick gazed through a gap in the fence, fluttering his tail feathers happily. The flamingos were perched in the middle of a shallow pond, each one balancing on one of their long legs, with the other leg tucked up underneath their bodies. Their feathers were a pretty pink color, and their slender necks and heads a slightly darker pink. Great-Uncle Horace had explained to Zoe that the brighter the color of a flamingo, the healthier and happier it was. All the birds at the Rescue Zoo were especially bright and beautiful!

The little penguin looked up at Zoe hopefully and gave a little peep.

Zoe had to smile. "Yes, they are birds like you," she admitted, "but they're a different type of bird. You're definitely not a flamingo, Pip."

Pip stared at the pink birds and cheeped stubbornly.

Zoe smiled down at him. "OK, Pip. We can go inside if you want. But I promise you're a penguin!"

She unlocked the gate using her paw-print charm and walked in, followed by Meep and Pip. All at the same time, the flamingos swiveled around to look at Zoe and squawked a friendly greeting. One of them stalked gracefully up to the edge of the pond and gently nuzzled Zoe with her beak. She was one of the smallest birds, with a splash of black among the pink feathers above her beak.

"Hi, Fifi," Zoe began, "this is Pip. He arrived yesterday with Great-Uncle Horace." She hesitated, not sure how to explain Pip's problem.

Meep piped up. "But he thinks he might be a flamingo!"

Pip peeped enthusiastically and flapped his wings.

75

"So we wondered," continued Zoe, "if you could show him what flamingos do?"

The flamingo looked at the little chick curiously, but bobbed her long neck up and down in agreement.

Fifi stepped out of the pond and bent her neck down low, so that she could speak to the little chick. Zoe and Meep both giggled to see Pip standing with the tall, slender, colorful flamingos. The tiny chick looked nothing like Fifi and her family!

"I wonder what Fifi's saying," Zoe whispered to Meep.

They soon found out. Pip watched carefully as Fifi raised one leg up and tucked it away underneath her feathery body. The flamingo nodded kindly, and Pip lifted one of his webbed orange feet up. The little chick wobbled — and fell

right over on his
fluffy bottom!
    Meep
collapsed
on the
ground,
giggling.
    "Meep!" Zoe
scolded. "Don't
laugh at poor Pip."
She rushed over to help
Pip to his feet. The little penguin shook
himself and cheeped sadly as he waddled
away from the water.

    Zoe smiled gently. "No, I don't think
you're a flamingo either, Pip. Come on,
let's try somewhere else. Thank you for
helping us, Fifi."

    Fifi squawked good-bye.

77

"Don't worry," Meep chirped. "We won't let you fall over again, Pip. Which animal should we visit next?"

The little chick cheeped excitedly and rushed forward again. Zoe had to try very hard not to laugh when she saw which enclosure Pip was heading for this time.

"The zebras!" squeaked Meep. "Zoe, does Pip really think he might be a zebra? They're not even birds!"

"I think it must be because they're black and white," said Zoe, smiling. "Come on, Meep. Let's go and say hello to Cleo."

Pip cheeped eagerly, and Zoe scooped him up. Meep leaped onto her shoulder and curled his furry tail around her neck. Zoe opened the gate with her paw-print necklace and walked inside. The enclosure was a huge stretch of warm, rocky forest, dotted with star chestnut and acacia trees.

The zebras were in the middle of eating a big pile of golden hay and a mound of carrots. When they saw Zoe, they all whinnied and snorted to say hello. Cleo trotted over shyly. She had the most beautiful striped coat of jet black and pure white. Her huge, shiny black eyes were framed with long lashes. Zoe stroked her muzzle gently. It felt like it was made of soft, warm velvet.

Zoe introduced Pip to Cleo and explained the problem.

Cleo snorted gently and trotted back to where the rest of her family were munching away. She pulled up a big mouthful of hay and brought it over, placing it carefully at Pip's feet.

Pip looked at the pile of hay
uncertainly. He glanced up at Zoe and
cheeped. Zoe giggled. "Zebras don't eat
fish, Pip. This is called hay. It's what
zebras eat. Would you like to try some?"

The little penguin shook his head and
cheeped again, sadly this time. "I don't
think you're a zebra either, Pip," Zoe said
gently. "Nevermind."

They said good-bye and left the
enclosure. As they walked back on to

the path, the tiny chick waddled along very slowly, making an unhappy peeping noise. Zoe knelt down to stroke his little belly. "Don't be sad, Pip," she whispered.

As they trooped along, Will rushed past, clutching a stack of colorful papers and a packet of adhesive putty. "There you are, Zoe!" he said. "Has little Pip been behaving himself? I've made some posters for the penguin-feeding show, so I'm just going to stick a few up around the zoo." He waved the papers in the air. "How are the ticket sales going today?" he added hopefully.

Zoe gasped. *The tickets!* She had meant to go to the hut after bringing Pip to meet the colony, but she had been so busy trying to help the little chick, she had completely forgotten!

Chapter Nine
The Show is Canceled

Zoe felt awful. How could she have forgotten about the penguin show? She knew she had let Will down. The show was his idea, and he wanted it to be a big success.

"I'm really sorry, Will," she muttered. "I haven't sold any."

Will's face fell, but he tried not to look

too disappointed. "That's all right, Zoe," he said. "I know you've been taking care of Pip this morning. We'll just cancel today's show. It doesn't matter."

Zoe nodded. "Thanks for being so nice, Will," she said quietly. "I won't forget again."

"Don't worry," Will reassured her. "I'm sure you'll sell lots tomorrow! Now, maybe we should put up a sign to let visitors know the show isn't on today?"

Will pulled a pen out of his pocket and scribbled a note on the back of a poster. SHOW CANCELED TODAY. PLEASE COME TOMORROW FOR PENGUIN FUN! "There," he said. "Let's go and stick it up on the hut."

Zoe followed Will miserably back to the penguin enclosure. Just as they were

putting the sign in place, Meep squeaked
a warning. A moment later, Zoe heard
the click of Mr. Pinch's shoes coming
down the path, and her heart sank. The
grumpy zoo manager was *not* going to be
happy about this.

"I thought I'd come and check on the
ticket sales," announced
Mr. Pinch as he strolled
over to them. "Only
twenty-three sold
yesterday,"
he added,
looking
at Zoe.
"Not very
impressive,
Miss Parker."

Zoe glanced nervously at Will, who cleared his throat. "Well, Mr. Pinch . . . you see . . ."

Before Will could explain what had happened, Mr. Pinch spotted the sign on the side of the hut. His eyes narrowed and he stepped closer to read it. "Canceled? What is the meaning of this?"

"It's my fault," Zoe burst out. "I was looking after Pip . . ."

"Pip?" snapped Mr. Pinch. "Who's Pip?"

The tiny penguin heard his name and peeped.

Mr. Pinch glanced down and spotted the chick huddled behind Zoe's legs. Zoe watched as Mr. Pinch's mouth dropped open. "*What* is that creature doing outside its enclosure?" he spluttered.

Will jumped in quickly. "Zoe's been

helping me out with the new arrival and
doing a fantastic job. Little Pip's finding it
hard to settle in with the other penguins,
you see."

Mr. Pinch interrupted Will. "*I* find
it difficult to believe that a penguin
would find it hard to settle in with other
penguins!" he barked. He pointed an
angry finger at Zoe. "You have one more
chance. Tomorrow's show had better be
sold out, or I'm holding you responsible."

He turned to Will. "Now, please take
that penguin back to its enclosure
immediately. I will not have animals
running wild and making the zoo look
disorganized!"

"Yes, Mr. Pinch," Will said, looking very
flustered. "Come along, Pip." He tried to
pick up the little chick, but Pip cheeped

anxiously and waddled over to Zoe, his tiny wings stretched out toward her.

"I'm sorry, Pip," Zoe whispered quickly. "You have to go with Will now, but I'll come back tomorrow, I promise!"

As Mr. Pinch stormed off, Will managed to scoop Pip gently into his arms and carry him back inside the penguin enclosure. Both of them looked very miserable.

"Don't listen to horrible old Mr. Pinch, Zoe!" Meep whispered. "We'll sell lots of tickets tomorrow!"

Zoe smiled gratefully at her little friend. *Meep's right*, she thought. *I'll work extra hard at selling the tickets, even if it means missing out on all the fun this summer.* She bit her lip as she thought about Pip. *But helping the little chick is going to be even more difficult now.*

As they turned a corner next to the chipmunk enclosure, they both heard the sudden roar of an engine spluttering to life. "Zoe, it's coming from the lake. It's Goo's plane!" chirped Meep, leaping onto her shoulder.

They looked up at the sky, Zoe holding her hand up to her eyes to shield them from the bright sunshine. Great-Uncle Horace's red seaplane appeared over the tops of the trees, soaring high into the air on its way to the Great Barrier Reef. They waved frantically, and Zoe hoped Great-Uncle Horace would look

down over
the zoo
and spot
them. *I won't
let you down,
Great-Uncle Horace,*
Zoe thought fiercely. *I will help Pip.*

Meep must have been thinking the same thing. "Maybe we should take Pip to visit some more animals tomorrow," he suggested.

Zoe sighed. "Mr. Pinch is going to be keeping an eye on us tomorrow though, Meep. We need to sell lots of tickets. And I don't know if taking Pip to meet any more animals will help. Pip realized that he wasn't a flamingo or a zebra, but that still didn't make him see that he's a penguin."

Meep nodded his head.

"I think the chick is trying to
find something he loves," Zoe said
thoughtfully. "Once he does, he'll know
where he belongs."

Meep started bouncing excitedly on
her shoulder. "Swimming!" he chattered.
"That's what penguins love best, Zoe!"

"Meep, that's it!" Zoe cried. "Pip still
hasn't tried the most important thing
about being a penguin. That's what we've
got to do — make him try swimming!"

Meep thought of something. "But how?
We tried to get Pip to go for a swim this
morning, and he didn't want to! If he
won't try it, how will he know he likes it?"

"Meep," Zoe declared happily, "I think I
have an idea!"

Chapter Ten
Zoe Goes Swimming!

When Zoe and Meep went downstairs
for breakfast the next day, Zoe's mom
was putting a plate of toast and a jar of
jam on the kitchen table. As soon as she
saw Zoe, she started laughing. "What
on earth are you doing, Zoe?" she cried.
"You're dressed for a day at the beach,
not the zoo!"

Zoe grinned as she spread jam on a piece of toast. She was wearing her pink-and-white wetsuit that she always wore when she went swimming in the chilly lake and a pair of bright-pink flip-flops. Perched on her head was a pair of goggles. Under her arm she carried two yellow swimmies.

"I'm going swimming today — with the penguins!" she explained, taking a big, jammy bite of her toast. "I had an idea last night, and I think I might be able to help Pip. The little chick has to try swimming with the rest of the colony. He followed me everywhere yesterday. Maybe if I jump in first and show him how easy and fun it is, he might jump in after me!"

Zoe's mom beamed at her daughter.

"That's an excellent idea, Zoe. Sometimes our new arrivals do need a little bit of extra help to help them settle in!"

Zoe smiled, pleased that her mom liked the plan. She finished her toast and stood up. "Come on, Meep. Let's go down to the penguin enclosure right away. Hopefully, Mr. Pinch will still be eating his breakfast. We can't let him catch us there!"

When they arrived at the penguin enclosure, Zoe and Meep peered through the glass wall. A large proportion of the colony was perched on the rocks, chattering away. Some of the penguins were already leaping in and out of the lagoon, gliding through the cool blue water.

93

"Where's Pip, Zoe?" whispered Meep. "I can't see him anywhere."

Zoe glanced around the enclosure and spotted the tiny little chick. He was all by himself, huddled sadly at the very edge of the rocks. Zoe felt tears spring to her eyes. Pip looked so lonely.

As soon as Pip spotted them, he flapped his wings and cheeped happily.

"We're back!" Meep chirped as they rushed over.

Zoe gathered the penguin into her arms for a cuddle. Pip snuggled up against her.

"Why are you standing all alone?" Zoe asked him softly. "You should be with the rest of the birds. Look, they're all chatting and playing together. Don't you think that looks like fun?"

Pip gazed at Zoe and cheeped again, very seriously. Zoe giggled and shook her head. "You stood by yourself because you think you might be an owl? I don't think so, Pip. Owls are *nocturnal*. That means they sleep during the daytime and get up at night. It's definitely daytime now, and you're wide awake!" She gently stroked the little bird's fluffy belly. "Anyway, I think I know something that's going to make you feel like a penguin!"

Just then, Will came out of the little supply room at the back of the enclosure, holding that morning's bucket of krill for the penguins' breakfast. Pip saw the bucket and started wriggling around in excitement. Zoe laughed and placed him back on the ground. "Come on, Pip," she told him. "Let's go and get you something to eat."

Will waved as he saw them and looked curiously at Zoe. "Morning, Zoe! Er . . . you do know you're wearing your wetsuit, don't you?"

Zoe giggled and explained her idea to Will. The penguin-keeper smiled. "Fantastic idea, Zoe. I'll keep my fingers crossed!"

He dropped two tiny krill into Pip's beak. The penguin gobbled them up and peeped gratefully at Will.

"Funny, isn't it, Zoe?" chuckled Will,

offering him another tiny krill. "It almost sounds like Pip is saying thank you."

Zoe smiled at Will and winked at Meep. That's *exactly* what Pip had been saying!

When Pip had gobbled up a few more krill, Will picked up the bucket and began throwing silvery handfuls to the rest of the colony. With cheeps and squawks of excitement, the penguins rushed over to catch the krill in their flippers and beaks.

Gently, Zoe knelt down next to Pip. "Look at all the other penguins!" she whispered, making sure that Will was too busy feeding the other birds to hear her. "Do you see how much they're enjoying their breakfast? They all *love* fish — just like you. Fish is a penguin's favorite thing to eat!"

Meep nodded wisely from Zoe's shoulder. "Liking fish is one way to tell that you're a penguin, Pip!" the little lemur chattered helpfully.

"Another way to tell is by going swimming. Penguins love to swim more than anything," Zoe added. "And I'm going to have a little swim right now!"

Meep squealed and sprang off Zoe's shoulder. He scampered quickly away from the lagoon and found a smooth, dry patch of rock to perch on. Meep hated getting wet.

Zoe stood up and pulled her bright-yellow swimmies on. She had been to swimming lessons, but she wasn't as good at going underwater as the penguins. The inflatable armbands would help her stay afloat! She put on the goggles, stepped out of her pink flip-flops, and walked carefully toward the edge. Behind her, Pip waddled a little bit closer too. The penguin glanced uncertainly at the water, but he wanted to stay near Zoe.

The lagoon stretched out ahead of her, as perfectly smooth as a huge mirror, and sparkled in the morning sunlight. It was beautiful, but it looked *very* cold. Zoe took a deep, determined breath. *Please let this work*, she thought, and closed her eyes.

With a big splash, she leaped into the lagoon. As she landed in the icy water, she gasped. Even with her wetsuit on, it was colder than she had imagined!

From the edge of the lagoon, Will shouted, "Keep swimming, Zoe. You'll warm up!" Meep cheered from his rocky seat, bouncing up and down. Even Pip peeped excitedly and waddled forward a little bit more. Zoe lifted up both arms to wave at him and began to swim in a circle around the lagoon.

Suddenly, Poppy realized that Zoe was in the water. With an excited squawk, she called out to the rest of the colony. They whipped around to see. All at once, the penguins raced to the edge of the lagoon and dived right in to join Zoe! She giggled as they swooped right underneath her.

Pip was getting closer and closer to the lagoon edge. The chick looked interested now, but a little bit nervous too. Zoe glanced around quickly for the younger penguins. "Poppy! Pearl!" she whispered as loudly as she dared. "We need Pip to jump in. Let's all cheer for him!"

The penguins bobbed their sleek black heads up and down, then shot back through the water toward the edge of the lagoon. Zoe watched them cheeping encouragingly, and waving their flippers in the air. The rest of the colony copied them, and soon every single penguin was calling out to the little chick.

Zoe kicked her legs and swam closer to him. "Come on, Pip!" she called hopefully. "You'll love it. Jump in!"

Pip blinked his tiny dark eyes. Then he wriggled his fluffy little body bravely —

and jumped! With a *plop* and a *splash*, he landed in the lagoon. Zoe held her breath as he disappeared under the surface, and the other penguins dived underneath to watch. *What if I was wrong?* she thought suddenly, her heart racing. *What if he* doesn't *like swimming?* Her head was spinning with worry as she waited to see what Pip thought.

Suddenly, a tiny, pale-gray shape darted right past her toes. With a splash and a very excited peep, Pip's head popped above the surface of the lagoon! His feathery wings were fluttering so quickly, they were almost a blur.

"Pip!" Zoe cried. "You did it!"

The little chick peeped again and plunged back under the water, turning a nimble somersault before gliding away through the lagoon. Zoe had never seen him look so happy. It was as though Pip had been swimming for years instead of just a few minutes! The rest of the colony followed, swooping along after him. As they shot through the water, they left thousands of bubbles behind them, like streams of pearls.

Meep bounced so excitedly he nearly fell off his rock, and Will cheered. "Wonderful, Zoe!" he called. "Your plan worked! I'm going to radio your mom so she can come and see!"

Will disappeared into a small room at the back of the enclosure, grinning. Suddenly Zoe jumped and giggled. Something soft and fluffy was tickling her toes under the water! Then there was a tiny splash as Pip shot up and appeared right in front of her, cheeping happily.

Zoe laughed. "You're swimming, Pip!" she exclaimed in delight. "Now do you believe you're a penguin?"

The chick cheeped again and flapped his tiny wings excitedly. His eyes were bright, and his tail feathers were wagging happily. Zoe beamed, relief flooding through her. Her plan had worked. Pip *loved* swimming — and finally, he knew where he belonged!

Chapter Eleven
A Very Special Ice Pop

Pip swam through the lagoon, diving right down to the bottom and then shooting all the way back up to the surface. He wriggled his body to pick up speed, swimming faster and faster . . . and then leaped right out of the water, sailing through the air before splashing back in again!

Zoe heard a voice gasp, "Oh, wow! Look, Mom — there's a girl swimming with the penguins!"

Zoe looked through the glass wall of the enclosure. The zoo gates must have just opened, as visitors were streaming down the path. As people spotted Zoe in the lagoon, they rushed over to watch. Lots of visitors pulled out their cameras and snapped photos of her, and Zoe waved at them shyly. Will came back out into the enclosure and settled down on the rocks next to Meep, looking pleased with all the attention.

Suddenly Zoe froze. Behind the crowd of happy people she saw one very angry face coming down the path toward her. Mr. Pinch looked even angrier than yesterday. He pushed rudely through the visitors, scowling furiously at Zoe.

"Miss Parker, this is a disgrace!" he snapped. "Is *this* your idea of selling tickets for the penguin-feeding show?"

The crowd of visitors turned to stare at Zoe curiously. Zoe could feel her cheeks turning pink. *The tickets*, she thought. *I'm in so much trouble.*

Then she felt something very small and soft brushing against her hand. She looked down. Pip rubbed his head against her, making a very happy peeping sound. Zoe couldn't help smiling at the little chick. *I did the right thing*, she thought. *I don't mind getting into trouble with Mr. Pinch, if that's what it takes to help Pip. But . . . maybe I can still do something to help Will and the show too!*

Zoe splashed across to the glass wall so that she could speak to the crowd over the top of it. "Hello, everyone!" she called. "My name is Zoe. As you can see, we have lots of beautiful penguins here at the Rescue Zoo. Most of our birds are Adélie, rock hopper, or emperor penguins. They're all *very* friendly — including the colony's newest member!"

She pointed to Pip. The little chick twittered excitedly and dived under the water, gliding toward Zoe. As he reached her, he popped up above the surface again, right in front of the crowd. "He's *adorable*," whispered a lady with curly white hair, lifting her granddaughter up to see better.

"This is Pip," Zoe explained to the crowd. "He arrived at the Rescue Zoo two days ago, and he loves his new home already! If any of you would like to see more of Pip and the other birds, there will be a special penguin-feeding show at three o'clock today." She glanced at Mr. Pinch's furious face and took a deep, nervous breath. "Would anyone like to buy a ticket?"

A little girl with a black braid was the first to reply. "Me, me!" she called eagerly.

Her mom smiled and nodded. "We'll take two!" she said. "These penguins are just so adorable."

Behind them, more people in the crowd nodded and called out. "Where can we buy our tickets?" asked a blonde lady wearing lots of pink lipstick.

"There's a little wooden hut on the other side of the path," Zoe told them, pointing. "That's where the tickets and the money box are. If you don't mind waiting just a couple of minutes, I'll jump out of the water and get dry. Then I'll come right over!"

The blonde lady tutted. "But you're having so much fun in the water. It seems such a shame to make you get out now!"

She turned to Mr. Pinch. "Excuse me," she said bossily. "I think I heard *you* say something about the show before. Why does this little girl have to sell the tickets? We can just put our money directly into the box and take a ticket ourselves. That seems much simpler to me."

The crowd murmured in agreement. Mr. Pinch stared in disbelief at the crowd. Before he could argue, the blonde lady reached into her handbag for her wallet and marched over to the hut. The rest of the crowd followed her, eagerly chatting about the show. Shaking his head angrily, the zoo manager shot a final glare at Zoe and stomped after them.

Zoe couldn't believe it. Will grinned at her. "Fantastic, Zoe!" he said. "You don't have to spend the whole summer in the

111

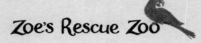

hut — the visitors are going to buy hundreds of tickets!"

"In fact, it looks as though today's show is going to sell out!" called another voice. Zoe turned to see her mom stepping into the enclosure, holding a big, fluffy white towel under one arm and a small box under the other. "I just walked past the hut," she continued. "There's a line of visitors stretching all the way to the hippo enclosure!"

Zoe splashed to the edge of the lagoon and climbed out, dripping and shivering. Zoe's mom wrapped the soft white towel around her shoulders. Zoe cuddled into it gratefully.

"Now, you go and sit in the sunshine with Meep," her mom told her. "You'll be warm and dry in just a few minutes, and then I've got a treat for you both."

Zoe stepped into her flip-flops and went to sit by her best friend. She started to feel warmer right away. As she tipped her head back to enjoy the sunshine on her face, Meep leaped into her lap for a hug. "Meep, I'm still wet!" Zoe said, laughing. "You know you'll be grumpy if your fur gets damp."

"I don't mind," Meep chirped, nuzzling his head against her. "I'm too excited, Zoe. Pip's happy, and we get a treat!"

"Even better, we don't have to sell any more tickets!" Zoe added, grinning as her little friend started jumping up and down in excitement. "I can't believe it, Meep. We've got our summer back!"

They sat in the sun for a little while, watching the penguins swoop and glide in the lagoon. Zoe changed back into her summer dress and was soon dry and warm again.

"Here you go, you two!" her mom called. "Come and have something yummy for a hot summer's day."

Zoe made her way back over to the edge of the lagoon, with Meep scampering eagerly ahead. Zoe's mom opened the little box and held it out to them. "There's a strawberry ice pop for you, Zoe, and some frozen mango for Meep," she said.

"And I've got something special for the penguins too," added Will, bringing out a larger box. He smiled proudly as he took the lid off and showed them what was inside. "Fish ice pops! I made them last night, from frozen sardines. Zoe, will you help me hand them out?"

Zoe reached into the box and picked up a handful of the cold, slippery ice pops. As the penguins started splashing out of the water and waddling over to her, she placed them on the ice so that they could nibble and peck away at them. Zoe made sure that Pip had a big ice pop all to himself. "Eat it all up, Pip!" she whispered. "You've done lots of swimming this morning. You must be very hungry!"

They heard a snooty voice behind them. "Well, it looks as though the penguin-feeding show is going to be a very popular attraction at the Rescue Zoo after all! I knew all along that it was one of my best ideas."

Zoe whirled round to see Mr. Pinch looking very smug. Will cleared his throat. "Er, Mr. Pinch. Actually, it was *my* —"

Mr. Pinch continued loudly. "Yes, a truly excellent idea." He spotted the fish ice pops in Zoe's hand. "So if anyone deserves to relax with an ice pop, it really should be me."

Before Zoe could stop him, Mr. Pinch had grabbed one of the ice pops out of her hands and given it a big lick. Zoe's mom and Will both gasped, and Zoe held her breath.

Mr. Pinch chewed the ice pop thoughtfully. "Hmm . . . what an unusual flavor," he commented, taking another bite. "Is it . . . apple? Lemon? No, strawberry! No, that's not it . . ."

Zoe glanced at the others. Will was grinning and her mom was trying very hard not to smile!

"It's a special new flavor," Will told Mr. Pinch helpfully, winking at Zoe. "Homemade this morning to celebrate little Pip settling in so well."

Mr. Pinch nodded. "Very . . . interesting. Well, I'd better get going. I have a very busy day ahead, as usual."

They all watched Mr. Pinch as he disappeared down the path, still munching away at his fish ice pop. As soon as he was out of sight, everyone burst out laughing.

"That was the funniest thing I've seen in a long time!" said Will, shaking his head. "Well, it serves the old grump right for pretending the show was his idea!"

"Oh, dear — poor Mr. Pinch," added Zoe's mom, smiling. "I think we'd better keep this a secret, Zoe. He'd be so mad if he found out what was really in that ice pop!"

Zoe grinned and nodded. "I won't say a word," she promised. *But the next time Mr. Pinch shouts at me,* she thought, *I'll just*

remember him taking a giant slurp of sardine-flavored ice pop, and I'll feel much better!

As Pip and the other penguins finished their treats and started diving back into the lagoon, Will picked up the box. "I'd better go and put these spare ice pops back in the freezer before Mr. Pinch comes back and eats them all!" he said, winking.

"And I'd better get back to the hospital," Zoe's mom said, standing up. "One of the little bear cubs has hay fever. He's been sneezing all morning! Do you want to come, Zoe?"

"Can I stay here for a little bit longer?" Zoe asked.

Her mom smiled. "You can do anything you want," she said, ruffling Zoe's hair. "You've got the whole summer to spend at the zoo."

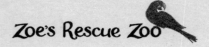

As her mom left the enclosure, Zoe sat back down on the edge of the lagoon to eat her ice pop, dangling her feet in the cool water. Meep jumped onto her shoulder, clutching a piece of mango in his tiny fingers. They both waved at Pip, who was splashing happily in the middle of the lagoon. The little chick flapped his flippers before swooping under the surface with some of his new friends.

Zoe licked her ice pop and sighed. "I'm so happy, Meep," she told her friend. "Pip's going to fit in perfectly at the Rescue Zoo. And now we can come and play with him everyday for the rest of the summer!"

Meep chirped in agreement. "And can we see Bella everyday too, Zoe?" he added hopefully. Bella was a gorgeous

polar bear cub who was just a few
months old and was one of Zoe and
Meep's special friends at the zoo.

"Definitely!" said Zoe. "And we can
give Oscar his breakfast every morning,
just like we promised him! I want to spend
lots of time with the baby wallabies and
the pygmy piglets too. And one night,
Mom said we could have a sleepover
under the stars and watch the snowy owls
flying above us. I can't wait!"

Meep squeaked in excitement and Zoe
scooped her little friend into her arms
for a cuddle. She sighed happily. "Meep,
I think this is going to be our best ever
summer at the Rescue Zoo!"